I love everything about:

_____

For my niece Zyla and all the girls who Dream Big.
—Fatima Scipio

To all the young girls who may need small reminders that they are GREAT!
—Paige Mason

Entangled Publishing, LLC
644 Shrewsbury Commons Ave., STE 181
Shrewsbury, PA 17361
rights@entangledpublishing.com

Little Lark is an imprint of Entangled Publishing, LLC.

Visit our website at www.entangledpublishing.com.

Book design by Bree Archer
The text for this book is set in Snicker
The illustrations for this book were created with watercolor, art pens, and Photoshop
Manufactured in China
ISBN 978-1-64937-438-7
Ebook ISBN 978-1-64937-439-4

Ebook Edition Also Available

First Edition September 2023

10 9 8 7 6 5 4 3 2 1

LITTLE
lark

I LOVE EVERYTHING ABOUT ME

I love everything, absolutely everything

about ME!

My eyes.

My cheeks.

My lips

and my teeth.

I LOVE EVERYTHING ABSOLUTELY EVERYTHING ABOUT ME!

My hair
when it's
straight.

Or kinky or curly.

At home or at school. At bedtime or early.

When I wear it
in braids

or a ballerina
bun.

Big bows for
my pigtails.

Pulled back when
I run.

I LOVE EVERYTHING ABOUT ME! I LOVE EVERYTHING ABSOLUTELY EVERYTHING ABOUT ME! I LOVE EVERYTHING ABSOLUTELY ABOUT ME! I LOVE EVERYTHING ABSOLUTELY EVERYTHING ABOUT ME! I LOVE EVERYTHING ABSOLUTELY EVERYTHING ABOUT ME!

When I sing in
the mirror

or play
my guitar.

Or look at the night sky

to find the North Star.

When I wear red

or blue

or pink

or green

yellow

or purple

or bright tangerine.

**When I'm
taking a hike.**

Or riding my bike.
Or eating the flavor
of ice cream I like.

When I'm caught
in the rain

or the wind starts
to blow.

When it's
icky-sticky hot

and the sun
is aglow.

Underwater with fishes.

Or helping wash dishes.

Or in the pool
floating

making big and
small wishes.

I LOVE

ABSOLUTELY

TELY

ABOUT

EVERYTHING

EVERYTHING

ME!

Like running through sprinklers on a hot summer day.

Or catching red bugs
until they fly away.

Like going to the park and playing hide-and-seek

on a scavenger hunt with my
friends at the creek.

On days at the beach when I play in the sand.

Or eat cotton candy from the cotton-candy stand...

I'm amazing.
Really amazing,
you see.

I LOVE EVERYTHING ABSOLUTELY

EVERYTHING ABOUT

ME!